Pearl

Molly Idle

Little, Brown and Company
New York   Boston

*I*n the vast sea of blue,
some mermaids watched over the waves
breaking upon the endless beaches.

Some kept an eye on the great coral reefs.

Some tended to the towering forests of kelp
rising from the ocean floor.

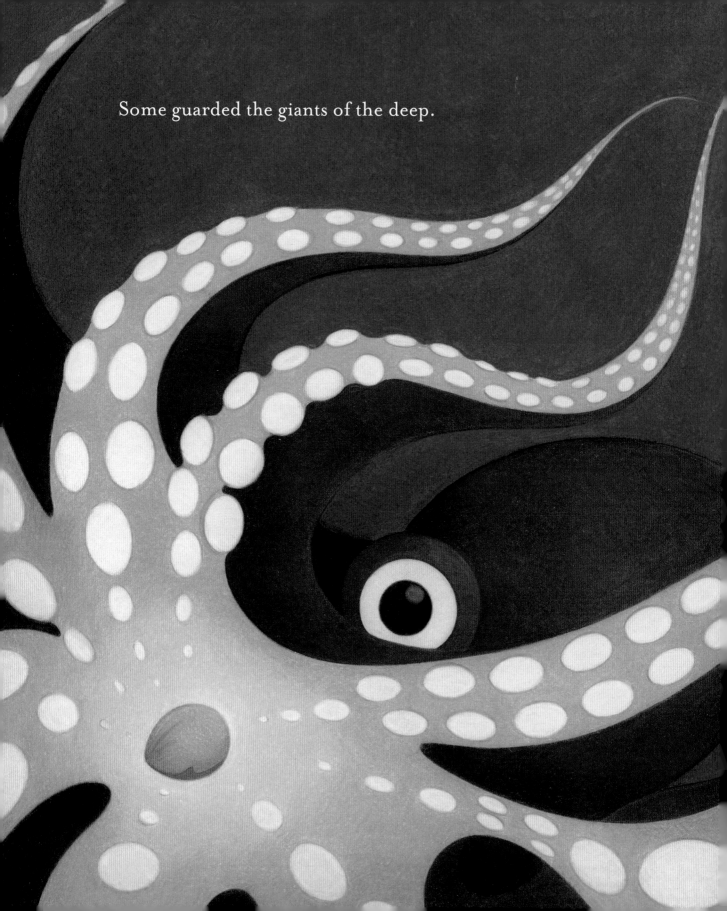

Some guarded the giants of the deep.

And Pearl deeply yearned to be one of them.

"Mother, I am big enough to help too," she said.

"Yes, Pearl." Her mother considered.
"Come with me.
I have something very important
for you to look after."

They swam up...

and up...

and up...

...past the breaking waves, until the sandy shore stretched all around them. "This," said her mother, "is yours."

She placed a single grain of sand in Pearl's hand.
"Yours, to care for every day and keep safe every night."

"But, Mother…" protested Pearl, "you said I could help
with something important."

"The smallest of things can make
a great difference, Pearl,"
her mother replied.

With that, Pearl was left alone.
A wave of disappointment washed over her.

She was surrounded by thousands of grains of sand...
millions...*billions* beyond counting!
And here she was entrusted with just one?

Her heart grew heavy,
and the weight of it pulled her
down...

down...

down...

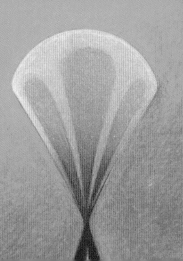

…where the salt of her tears mingled with the sea.

Pearl glowered at the grain of sand.
She clenched it in her tiny fist.

Then, from beneath her fingers,
came a faint light.

But when Pearl opened her hand, it was gone.

Pearl closed her hand around the tiny grain again... gently this time.

The sand resting on her palm had a luster to it that had not been there before.

polished it,

Every day, Pearl preserved it,

and played with it.

Every night she protected it.
And slowly, very slowly...
it began to grow.

And grow...

And *glow*.

and up…

And as it grew lighter, so did Pearl's heart.
It seemed to buoy them up…

and up...

...until it rose into the vast sea of stars.

Pearl beamed up at it.

It beamed back.

Its light touched everything.

It sparkled on the breaking waves
and the coral creating new reefs....

It glowed in the tides flowing through the towering forests and illuminated the giants rising from the deep....

And it shone

upon Pearl.

For Mr. Keane and Mr. Malk